Cubbie Blue and his Dog Dot-Book 3

Written and Illustrated

By Randa Handler

I See You!

As usual Derek, Christopher and Brian met at the bus stop. Cubbie and Dot were perched atop Derek's backpack and dissecting all the scenery near and far. As the school bus, approached their classmate Leo's house, they peered through the windows and watched the front door intensely. But, no sign of Leo. And the bus, pulled into their friend's driveway, made a U-turn and continued to school.

"Check it out! Four eyed Dumbo missed the bus again!" smirked their classmate David.

"Too busy eating breakfast," laughed another.

Cubbie frowned at that and shook his head disapprovingly. Dot looked annoyed too and was getting agitated. "Dotty Dot, leave them alone. They're just mean! We're not used to that. Actually, they remind me of the pesky Ariana soldiers," whispered Cubbie. "Mean, for sure, they're always calling Leo names. One time David, on purpose, slammed into Leo, and made him fall down the stairs," lamented Derek.

Together, the boys headed to their classroom with Cubbie bouncing atop the side of Derek's backpack.

"What's up with Leo? Sick?" worried Derek.

"I know. This is the second time he misses school," answered Brian.

"Did you notice the big bump on his forehead Monday?" asked Christopher.

"Yep, it was huge. That gotta hurt!" replied Derek.

"Do you want me to check it out? Do you want Dot to sniff around there?" urged Cubbie.

"Send me! Send me," volunteered Dot.

"Sssssssshhh, be quiet, you guys. Someone might hear you," whispered Brian.

Later in the classroom Derek tugged at Brian's sleeve and said, "Know what? I can't find my little radio."

"When did you have it last?" inquired Brian.

"Here at school. I remember Leo playing with it. I can't find it anywhere! Have you guys seen it?" continued Derek.

In unison, Christopher and Brian shook their heads in a "no" taking their classroom seats by Derek's. Dot yawned and climbed atop Derek's pencil.

"Don't worry, I'm invisible!" whispered Dot.

"Okay, but how can you sleep with me, writing?" puzzled Derek.

"Dot likes that. It's like being atop a floating ice block," answered Dot.

Two days later, Derek and Leo were seated next to each at their classroom computers. Leo was agitated and upset about something. Derek, flicked Dot off his pencil to wake him. Dot, wagged his tails and shook his four ears as if to get a better understanding of the situation. He squeaked alerting Cubbie who flew from Derek's backpack and onto Leo's head. Leo tried to kick him off as if he was a fly. Ignoring the two little creatures, Derek grabbed Leo's arm to calm him down. But, Leo became more agitated as their teacher asked,

"Leo, did you forget your homework again? Did you even do it?"

"My sister hid it from me. I will bring it tomorrow, I promise," replied Leo.

"Why would your sister do that?" frowned the teacher, but as Leo stared silently at his feet, she continued, "Okay, just don't forget it tomorrow! I am waiting for it!"

"Wow, Leo, why lie? You don't have a sister! She'll find out and you'll get in trouble," worried Derek.

"I will bring it tomorrow!" shrugged Leo, ignoring the question about lying.

Later that afternoon, Derek, Brian and Christopher decided to spend their break picking up recyclables from the school yard. "Why don't peee--ople reee--cycle?" lamented Christopher.

"And, why litter next to the trash bins?" huffed Brian.

"Recycling is very important! Less footprint! Scientists think that we can influence the climate too! We have been keeping an eye on our ecological footprint for centuries on Baltar!" chimed Cubbie.

"What do you mean? How can we influence what happens? Can we make it rain? Can we stop icebergs from melting?" puzzled Derek.

"Pollution climbs up in the atmosphere and gets stuck there. The lighter our footprint, the healthier the environment," continued Cubbie.

"The recent Covid19 pandemic proved it! People stayed home, cities were deserted and factories were closed. Guess what happened? The air got cleaner, wildlife, and our earth got happier," chimed Dot.

"Dot is right. Compare before and after photos of the big cities' skylines and you will see it clearly. Photos don't lie!" insisted Cubbie.

"Speaking of lying, why does Leo do it so much?" interrupted Brian.

"Did he lie about copying my drawing? Did he ab---out pinnnn---ning that silly noooo---te to my backpack?" echoed Christopher.

"How about my radio? Do you guys think, he took it?" worried Derek.

"Weird, right Dotty Dot? Fear? Attention?" wondered Cubbie.

"The truth never stays hidden forever, right, Coba?" whispered Dot.

"Why does Leo lie so much? Why is he always skipping school? I'll go to his house and check it out. I'll stay invisible," decided Cubbie.

"Yap, yap, Dotty Dot, will come along too. I need him to keep Coba out of trouble," jumped Dot.

"In the meantime, I'll take a little nap. Maybe, I will hear from Astra and get some news of those crazy nasty Ariana soldiers. Talk about creatures who constantly lie and are so unhappy!" yawned Cubbie, jumping into Dereck's backpack, followed by Dot.

That night, after dining on strawberries, Cubbie perched himself at Leo's bedroom window. He was about to fall asleep, when suddenly Dot wiggled out of his chest pocket pointing at the night stand. And, here it was, Derek's radio.

"Dotty Dot, he did steal it. That's so sad," whispered Cubbie.

"Yap, yap, let's tell the boys," huffed Dot.

They were about to climb into the bubble and fly back when they hear Leo's mom yell, "Leo, come here, this instant!"

"Ah! The head bump," whispered Cubbie, observing Leo bang his head against the wall.

"I am coming mom!" answered Leo, in a trembling voice.

"No, oh no! I don't like what's about to happen," sniffed Dot.

Tightly holding on to Dot, Cubbie intently waited. Leo was about to go downstairs, when instead, his mom swings the door open, cell phone in hand. "Sister? What sister? Enough with the lying, enough," she yelled. Leo's cries and protests, were met with a stern, "No dinner, tonight, understand? That would teach you to lie again!"

"Oh, Dotty Dot. It's sad that she doesn't talk to him instead. Does anyone see what he's going through?" lamented Cubbie.

"Dot, is still uneasy. Something else is coming, Coba," sniffed Dot.

"What else can happen to poor Leo? What do you see?" sighed Cubbie.

"We better wait a bit longer, Coba!" retorted Dot.

They waited and observed Leo lift his mattress, and grab a candy filled plastic bag. "Halloween leftover bounty?" thought Cubbie.

The next day, Derek, Brian and Christopher worriedly watched the bus climb into Leo's driveway. The bus driver waited a few minutes but Leo was a no show.

"Four eyed Dumbo is still eating everyone's breakfast!" giggled David, slurping his orange soda.

"Can't stand it! Can't," squeaked Dot, fluttering toward David, messing up his hair with his tails. David tried to shoo him away, spilling his soda all over his chest.

The entire bus laughed in unison which annoyed David.

That night, the boys decided to camp, in a tent, in Derek's backyard. They each brought snacks to share and strawberries for their little friends.

"Leo must have gotten sick eating all that candy! We will help him with the binge eating. Too bad he doesn't like strawberries. So, delicious! We'll all get him to stop lying, right, Dot?" beamed Cubbie.

The tent turns the color of blue. The boys smiled, as that meant Cubbie was dreaming, focusing or assessing things.

"What… wh--at ca--n we do?" stuttered Christopher.

"Let me see…" thought and thought, pensively Brian.

Everyone waited but as usual Brian added, "Got nothing!"

"Bri-an! Ev-er gon-na stop th-at!" stuttered Christopher.

"Calm down, Chris! Breathe in, count til five and breathe out, count til five, okay? We'll come up with something!" smiled Derek, tapping Christopher on the shoulder.

"Together, we'll figure it out!" rushed Cubbie, tickling Christopher with his beard, making him giggle.

"I will watch him tonight and I will find out what to do," said Cubbie.

"Dot better tag along to keep you safe," snapped Dot.

Leo's was asleep when Cubbie perched himself at his window.

"Dot, I got it! I will make Leo have a weird dream tonight! He will be convinced that once candy hits his stomach, it comes alive! Maybe, that will make him think twice before binging on junk food and candy!" concluded Cubbie, his fingers tapping to an inner beat. Dot closed his eyes, flattening ears and tails in deep concentration.

Leo starts tossing and turning as Cubbie and Dot concentrated and concentrated. A little magic dust and Pouf, "Mission accomplished!" exclaimed Cubbie.

Back on Baltar, Astra was trying again to see Cubbie's image in her glass pyramid Zoner Locator.

"Dotty Dot, where are you? You usually track me, sonically! Are you with Coba? Are you okay? Can you hear me?" she pleaded into her Locator.

Wiping her tears, she focused, again and again, but the Locator would fog up without any images. "I will keep trying to zone you. I'm sure you heard me even if I can't see you nor hear you. The Ariana soldier twirled back to Ariana without their ponytails. Coba, you cut them, right? My alerts about their ponytails 'connection to their powers reached you, right?" laughed Astra.

Dot yanked Cubbie's beard, waking him, as Leo's bedroom turned the color of blue. "An Astra dream?" he asked. Leo was about to freak out when Cubbie and Dot jumped over to say hello. After an initial scare, Leo relaxed, intrigued by his tiny visitors. "Let's make ourselves visible. He is lonely, sad and needs a friend, right?" Cubbie.

"Yap, yap, Leo has a good heart and we'll be safe," agreed Dot.

"Leo, we're different but have lots in common. Don't be afraid. Even though small, I am able to see deep into situations and people. I see YOU. I had my own share of timeouts! Sometimes, I get too excited and do bad things. I have also binged at sugar rains," lamented Cubbie.

"Sugar rain? Wouldn't mind some of that," thought Leo.

"Yap, yap, me too. We're lost, because of wrong decisions," snapped Dot.

"Are you guys okay?" worried Leo.

"We're fine now. We have three great giant new friends. We love learning about each other's special differences. We all go to your school," beamed Cubbie

"My school?" puzzled Leo.

"And, we'll be your friend too. Together will stand up to David. But, you have to tell the truth!" replied Cubbie.

"I don't know why I lie," shrugged Leo.

"Heard of the boy who cried wolf? What if, you needed help but no one came because they assumed you were faking! Easier to remember the truth than a lie, trust me! Why not think of your lucky baseball when tempted to take what isn't yours? Wouldn't you be upset if it was stolen?" continued Cubbie.

"Can you guys help me?" timidly asked Leo, grabbing and kissing his baseball.

Cubbie and Dot nodded in unison.

"We will. No more lying, okay? We promise to help you with junk food cravings too!" promised Cubbie, observing Leo rub his stomach as if to ease an upset.

"Oh, I think I'm okay there! Thinking of sweets is making me sick. I feel like that candy I devoured, last night, is alive in my tommy and cramping me, weird right?" lamented Leo.

"Strange, for sure. Hey, maybe imagining thumping live candies, before eating them can help you cut down a bit on them," replied Cubbie.

"Oh!" mumbled Leo while rubbing his stomach.

Cubbie and Dot returned home and quickly jumped onto Derek's head. "So, how is Leo?" asked Brian.

"Okay! We made a new friend," replied Cubbie.

"Cool, but wh---yyy di---ddd he miiii---sss school sooo muuuch?" stuttered Christopher, then giggling at Dot's kisses.

"Leo preferred to stay away from David's bullying, but now that we have his back, he will start liking school," replied Cubbie.

"Good, we can use more friends. And, the more help the better spreading word about climate change!" beamed Derek.

"Beautiful! We shield Baltar to make it invisible whenever those Ariana bullies are near. Unfortunately, lately, the shield has been failing due to shifting and melting of too many icebergs. Light reflexology has diminished so much, "lamented Cubbie.

"Yap, yap, maybe we're destined to be nomads! Global warming is happening so fast, we're reaching a place of no return and light reflexology at zero, "squeaked Dot

"Hopefully, as humans, we will save our Albedo," sighed Cubbie.

"Consider yourself human?" puzzled lovingly Derek

"Al---beee---dooo?" stuttered Brian.

"That's what has stabilized Earth for millions of years. When polar ice reflects light, it's like diamonds. It reflects it back into space which, believe it or not, keeps our earth's temperature constant. When sections of icebergs melt, you fall into negative Albedo which affects our global climate," continued Cubbie.

"We will try to make a difference, but we're just kids," cried Derek.

"Greta is a young girl and she is making the world listen," beamed Dot.

"True, she is. Science has shown that industrial pollution, travels for miles and is stored high up in the atmosphere, changing climate and interfering with plant, animal and geological life cycles, "continued Cubbie.

A week later, Cubbie, Dot, Derek and Christopher were busy at their classroom computers when Leo walked in. They looked up at him and to their surprise, he waved, approaching them. He smiled, ear to ear, noticing that Cubbie and Dot's matching eye wear.

"Hi, there! It's such a beautiful day! Isn't it?" said Leo.

"Beautiful. Making sure I see it clearly," exclaimed Cubbie, focusing his eyeglasses. "Yap, yap," squeaked Dot.

"Hey, great to see you!" answered Derek, surprised by Leo's friendly attitude.

"Derek, thanks for lending me your radio!" continued Leo, handing over the radio to Derek.

Everyone smiled in silence.

Cubbie and Dot were happy to hear from Astra that the Wisemen devised their safest way back to Baltar. They needed to go to Alaska, during a brief time frame when the bubble can hover, without freezing, atop its icy mountains. From there, the Zoner Locators can track them and lead them home. In the meantime, new wonderful adventures, intriguing discoveries, cool colorful diverse friendships await.

End

www.ingramcontent.com/pod-product-compliance
Lightning Source LLC
Chambersburg PA
CBHW041032170626
46815CB00001B/61